HORRID HENRY'S
Injection

HORRID HENRY'S
Injection

Francesca Simon
Illustrated by Tony Ross

Orion
Children's Books

Horrid Henry's Injection **was originally published in** *Horrid Henry and the Secret Club,* **but appears here for the first time in a single volume with brand-new full-colour illustrations.**

ORION CHILDREN'S BOOKS

Horrid Henry's Injection first appeared in *Horrid Henry and the Secret Club*
First published in Great Britain in 1995 by Orion Children's Books
This Early Reader edition first published in Great Britain in 2019
by Hodder and Stoughton

1 3 5 7 9 10 8 6 4 2

Text © Francesca Simon, 1995
Illustrations © Tony Ross, 1995

The rights of Francesca Simon and Tony Ross to be identified as author and
illustrator of this work have been asserted.

A CIP catalogue record for this book is available from the British Library.

ISBN 978 1 5101 0622 2

Printed and bound in China

The paper and board used in this book are from well-managed forests and other
responsible sources.

FSC
www.fsc.org
MIX
Paper from
responsible sources
FSC® C104740

Orion Children's Books
An imprint of
Hachette Children's Group
Part of Hodder & Stoughton
Carmelite House
50 Victoria Embankment
London EC4Y 0DZ

An Hachette UK Company
www.hachette.co.uk
www.hachettechildrens.co.uk
www.horridhenry.co.uk

*For the brilliant composer
Gavin Higgins*

Look out for:

Don't Be Horrid, Henry!
Horrid Henry's Birthday Party
Horrid Henry's Holiday
Horrid Henry's Underpants
Horrid Henry Gets Rich Quick
Horrid Henry and the Football Fiend
Horrid Henry's Nits
Horrid Henry and Moody Margaret
Horrid Henry's Thank You Letter
Horrid Henry and the School Fair
Horrid Henry and the Zombie Vampire
Horrid Henry's Hike

There are many more Early Reader
titles available.

For a complete list visit horridhenry.co.uk
or hachettechildrens.co.uk

Contents

Chapter 1

"AAGGHHH"
"AAAGGGGHHH!!!!"
"AAAAAGGGGGGHHHHH!!!!"
The horrible screams came from
behind Nurse Needle's closed door.
Horrid Henry looked at his
younger brother Perfect Peter. Perfect
Peter looked at Horrid Henry. Then
they both looked at their father, who
stared straight ahead.

Henry and Peter were in
Dr Dettol's waiting room.

Moody Margaret was there. So were
Sour Susan, Anxious Andrew, Jolly
Josh, Weepy William, Tough Toby,
Lazy Linda, Clever Clare,
Rude Ralph and just about
everyone Henry knew.

They were all waiting for the terrible moment when Nurse Needle would call their name.

Today was the worst day in the
world. Today was – injection day.

Horrid Henry was not afraid of
spiders. He was not afraid of spooks.
He was not afraid of burglars, bad
dreams, squeaky doors and things
that go bump in the night. Only one
thing scared him.

Just thinking about . . . about . . .
Henry could barely even say the
word – INJECTIONS – made him
shiver and quiver and shake
and quake.

Nurse Needle came into the waiting room. Henry held his breath. "Please let it be someone else," he prayed. "William!" said Nurse Needle.

Weepy William burst into tears.
"Let's have none of that," said
Nurse Needle. She took him firmly
by the arm and closed the door
behind him.

"I don't need an injection!" said
Henry. "I feel fine."

"Injections stop you getting ill,"
said Dad. "Injections fight germs."

"I don't believe in germs,"
said Henry.
"I do," said Dad.
"I do," said Peter.
"Well, I don't," said Henry.

Dad sighed. "You're having an injection, and that's that."

Chapter 2

"I don't mind injections," said
Perfect Peter. "I know how
good they are for me."
Horrid Henry pretended he was an
alien who'd come from outer space
to jab earthlings.
"OWW!" shrieked Peter.

"Don't be horrid, Henry!"
shouted Dad.
"AAAAAAGGGGGHHHHHH!"
came the terrible screams from
behind Nurse Needle's door.
"AAAAAAGGGGGHHHHH!
NOOOOOOOO!"

Then Weepy William staggered out,
clutching his arm and wailing.
"Crybaby," said Henry.

"Just wait, Henry,"
sobbed William.
Nurse Needle came into
the waiting room.
Henry closed his eyes.
"Don't pick me," he begged
silently. "Don't pick me."
"Susan!" said Nurse Needle.

Sour Susan crept into
Nurse Needle's office.
"AAAAAAGGGGGHHHHHH!"
came the terrible screams.
"AAAAAAGGGGGHHHHH!
NOOOOOOO!"

Then Sour Susan dragged herself out,
clutching her arm and snivelling.
"What a crybaby," said Henry.
"Well, we all know about you,
Henry," said Susan sourly.

"Oh yeah?" said Henry. "You don't know anything."
Nurse Needle reappeared. Henry hid his face behind his hands.
I'll be so good if it's not me, he thought. Please, let it be someone else.

"Margaret!" said Nurse Needle.
Henry relaxed.
"Hey, Margaret, did you know the needles are so big and sharp they can go right through your arm?" said Henry.

Moody Margaret ignored him and marched into Nurse Needle's office. Henry could hardly wait for her terrible screams. Boy, would he tease that crybaby Margaret!

Silence.

Then Moody Margaret swaggered into the waiting room, proudly displaying an enormous plaster on her arm. She smiled at Henry. "Ooh, Henry, you won't believe the needle she's using today," said Margaret. "It's as long as my leg."

"Shut up, Margaret," said Henry.
He was breathing very fast
and felt faint.

"Anything wrong, Henry?" asked
Margaret sweetly.
"No," said Henry. He scowled at her.
How dare she not scream and cry?

"Oh, good," said Margaret. "I just wanted to warn you because I've never seen such big fat whopping needles in all my life!"

Horrid Henry steadied himself.
Today would be different.
He would be brave.
He would be fearless.
He would march into Nurse
Needle's office, offer his arm, and
dare her to do her worst.
Yes, today was the day.

Brave Henry, he would
be called, the boy who laughed
when the needle went in, the boy
who asked for a second injection, the
boy who—

"Henry!" said Nurse Needle.
"NO!" shrieked Henry. "Please,
please, NO!"
"Yes," said Nurse Needle. "It's your
turn now."

33

Henry forgot he was brave.
Henry forgot he was fearless.
Henry forgot everyone
was watching him.
Henry started screaming and
screeching and kicking.

Chapter 3

"OW!" yelped Dad.
"OW!" yelped Perfect Peter.
"OW!" yelped Lazy Linda.
Then everyone started screaming
and screeching.

"I don't want an injection!"
shrieked Horrid Henry.
"I don't want an injection!"
shrieked Anxious Andrew.
"I don't want an injection!"
shrieked Tough Toby.
"Stop it," said Nurse Needle.
"You need an injection and an
injection is what you will get."
"Him first!" screamed Henry,
pointing at Peter.

"You're such a baby, Henry,"
said Clever Clare.
That did it.
No one ever called Henry a baby
and lived. He kicked Clare as hard as
he could. Clare screamed.

Nurse Needle and Dad each grabbed one of Henry's arms and dragged him howling into her office. Peter followed behind, whistling softly.

Henry wriggled free and dashed out. Dad nabbed him and brought him back. Nurse Needle's door clanged shut behind them.

Henry stood in the corner.
He was trapped.

Nurse Needle kept her distance. Nurse Needle knew Henry. Last time he'd had an injection he'd kicked her.

"Take a seat, Henry," said
Dr Dettol. Henry collapsed in a chair.
There was no escape.

"What a fuss over a little thing like an injection," said Dr Dettol. "Call me if you need me," she added, and left the room.

Henry sat on the chair, breathing hard. He tried not to look as Nurse Needle examined her gigantic pile of syringes.

But he could not stop himself peeking through his fingers. He watched as she got the injection ready, choosing the longest, sharpest, most wicked needle Henry had ever seen.

Then Nurse Needle approached,
weapon in hand.
"Him first!" shrieked Henry.
Perfect Peter sat down and rolled
up his sleeve.
"I'll go first," said Peter.
"I don't mind."

"Oh," he said, as he was jabbed.
"That was perfect," said
Nurse Needle.
"What a good boy you are," said Dad.
Perfect Peter smiled proudly.

Chapter 4

Nurse Needle rearmed herself.
Horrid Henry shrank back in the
chair. He looked around wildly.
Then Henry noticed the row of
little medicine bottles lined up
on the counter.

Nurse Needle was filling her injections from them.
Henry looked closer. The labels read: "Do NOT give injection if a child is feverish or seems ill."

Nurse Needle came closer,
brandishing the injection.
Henry coughed.
And closer. Henry sneezed.
And closer. Henry wheezed and
rasped and panted.

Nurse Needle lowered her arm.
"Are you all right, Henry?"

"No," gasped Henry. "I'm ill. My chest hurts, my head hurts, my throat hurts."

Nurse Needle felt his sweaty forehead. Henry coughed again, a dreadful throaty cough.

"I can't breathe," he choked.
"Asthma."

"You don't have asthma,
Henry," said Dad.
"I do, too," said Henry, gasping
for breath.

Nurse Needle frowned.
"He is a little warm," she said.

"I'm ill," whispered Henry
pathetically. "I feel terrible."
Nurse Needle put down
her syringe.

"I think you'd better bring him back when he's feeling better," she said.

"All right," said Dad. He'd make
sure Henry's mother brought him
next time.

Chapter 5

Henry wheezed and sneezed, moaned and groaned, all the way home. His parents put him straight to bed.

"Oh, Mum," said Henry, trying to sound as weak as possible. "Could you bring me some chocolate ice cream to soothe my throat? It really hurts."

"Of course," said Mum.
"You poor boy."

Henry snuggled down in the cool sheets. Ahh, this was the life.

"Oh, Mum," added Henry,
coughing. "Could you bring up the
TV? Just in case my head stops
hurting long enough for
me to watch?"
"Of course," said Mum.

Boy, this was great! thought Henry.
No injection! No school tomorrow!
Supper in bed!

There was a knock on the door. It must be Mum with his ice cream. Henry sat up in bed, then remembered he was ill. He lay back and closed his eyes.

"Come in, Mum," said Henry
hoarsely.
"Hello, Henry."
Henry opened his eyes. It wasn't
Mum. It was Dr Dettol.

Chapter 6

Henry closed his eyes and had a
terrible coughing fit.
"What hurts?" said Dr Dettol.

"Everything," said Henry. "My head, my throat, my chest, my eyes, my ears, my back and my legs."

"Oh dear," said Dr Dettol.

She took out her stethoscope and listened to Henry's chest. All clear.

She stuck a little stick in his mouth
and told him to say "AAAAAH."
All clear.

She examined his eyes and ears,
his back and his legs.
Everything seemed fine.

"Well, Doctor?" said Mum.
Dr Dettol shook her head. She
looked grave.

"He's very ill," said Dr Dettol.
"There's only one cure."

"What?" said Mum.
"What?" said Dad.

"An injection!"

Discover more Horrid Henry Early Readers: